For Brian and Daphne

First published 1988 by
Walker Books Ltd
87 Vauxhall Walk
London SE11 5HJ

Reprinted 1989, 1992

Printed and bound in Hong Kong by
South China Printing Co. (1988) Ltd

British Library Cataloguing in Publication Data
Dale, Penny
Ten in the bed.
I. Title
823'.914 [J]   PZ7
ISBN 0-7445-0797-9

TEN·IN·THE·BED

Penny Dale

WALKER BOOKS

LONDON

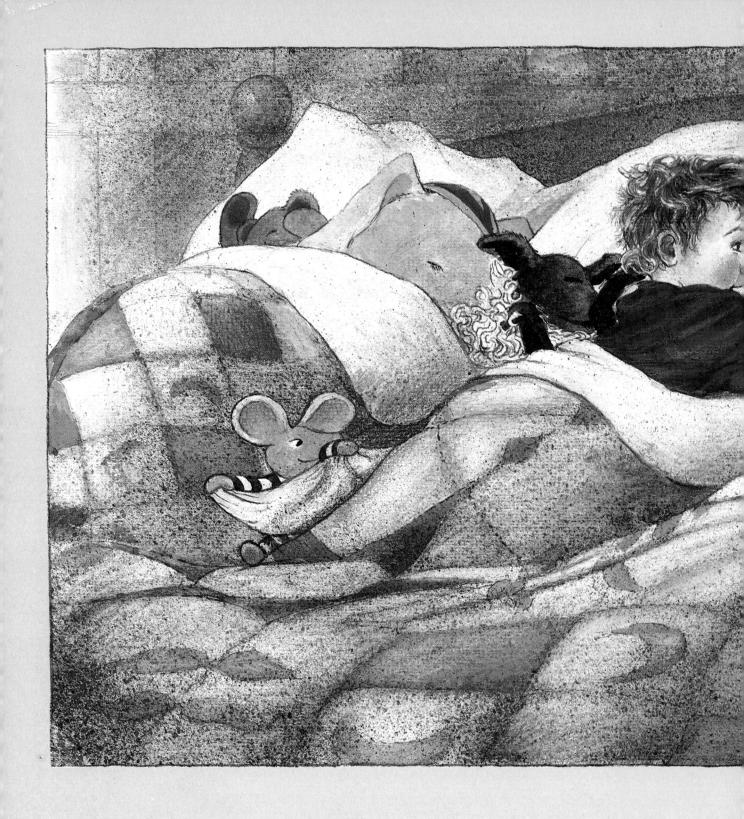

There were ten in the bed and the little one said,
"Roll over, roll over!"

So they all rolled over and Hedgehog fell out . . . BUMP!

There were nine in the bed and the little one said,
"Roll over, roll over!"
So they all rolled over and Zebra fell out . . . OUCH!

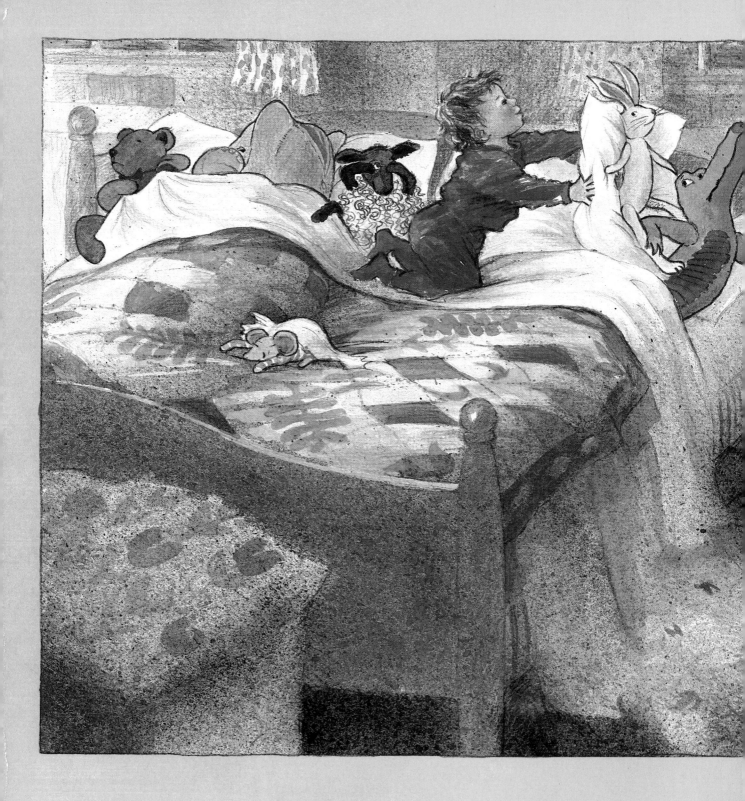

There were eight in the bed and the little one said,
"Roll over, roll over!"
So they all rolled over and Ted fell out . . . THUMP!

There were seven in the bed and the little one said,
"Roll over, roll over!"
So they all rolled over and Croc fell out . . . THUD!

There were six in the bed and the little one said,
"Roll over, roll over!"
So they all rolled over and Rabbit fell out . . . BONK!

There were five in the bed and the little one said,
"Roll over, roll over!"
So they all rolled over and Mouse fell out . . . DINK!

There were four in the bed and the little one said,
"Roll over, roll over!"
So they all rolled over and Nelly fell out . . . CRASH!

There were three in the bed and the little one said,
"Roll over, roll over!"
So they all rolled over and Bear fell out ... SLAM!

There were two in the bed and the little one said,
"Roll over, roll over!"
So they all rolled over and Sheep fell out . . . DONK!

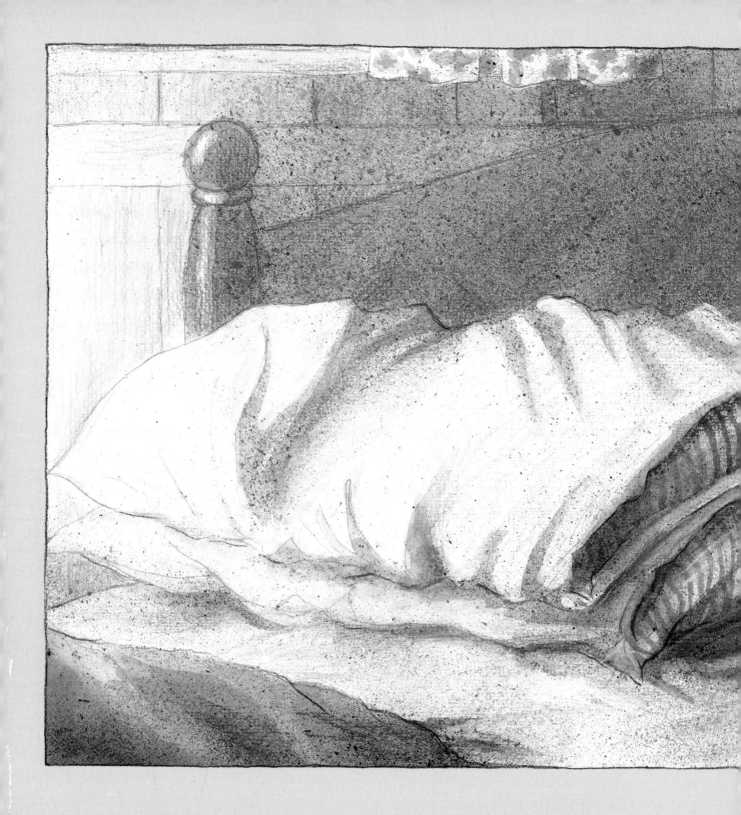

There was one in the bed and the little one said,

"I'm cold! I miss you!"

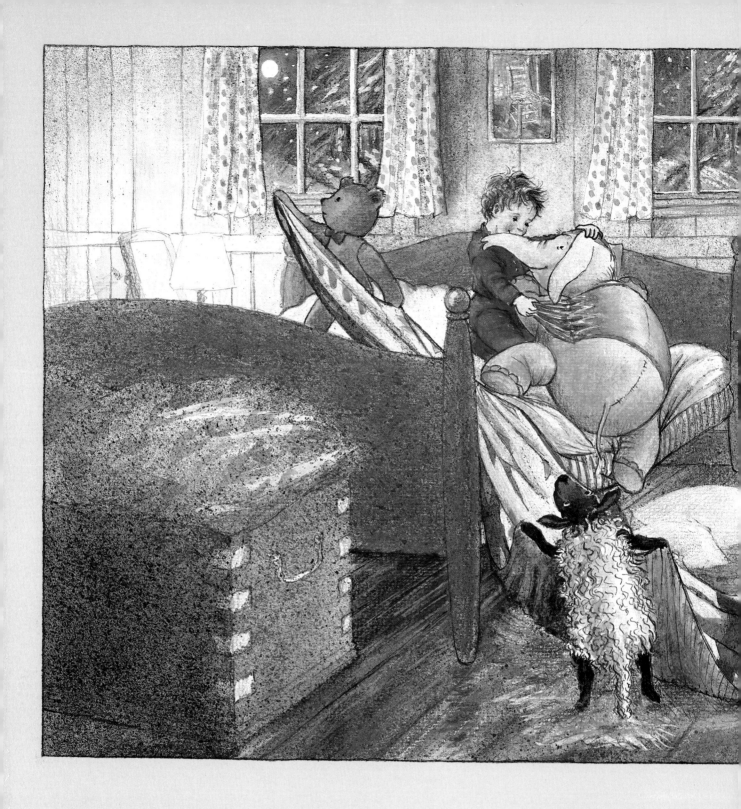

So they all came back . . .

and jumped into bed – Hedgehog, Mouse,
Nelly, Zebra, Ted,

the little one, Rabbit,
Croc, Bear and Sheep.

Ten in the bed, all fast asleep.

The End